Has Mandie found a pet?

SUDDENLY MANDIE HEARD a loud meow right behind her. It was a large black-and-white spotted cat, and it was looking up at her. She slowly reached down to pick it up.

"You found it!" Joe said.

"Yes, and I'm going to take it home with me," Mandie said, holding the animal tight. The cat's fur felt soft and warm in her hands.

"I don't know if that's a good idea," Joe said slowly.

"Why?"

"That cat is tame," Joe pointed out. "It must belong to somebody. And if you take it home with you, its owner will never find it."

Mandie frowned as she thought about this. "Well, if it belongs to someone, why is it lost here in the woods?"

D0066684

Don't miss any of Mandie Shaw's
page-turning mysteries!

And look for the next book, coming soon!

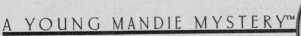

Who's Mandie?

Lois Gladys Leppard

BANTAM BOOKS
NEW YORK · TORONTO · LONDON · SYDNEY · AUCKLAND

Welcome to this world,
Olivia Joyce Loggia.

RL 2.6, ages 7–10
WHO'S MANDIE?
A Bantam Skylark Book / July 1999

Mandie® is a registered trademark of Lois Gladys Leppard.
A Young Mandie Mystery™ is a trademark of Lois Gladys Leppard.

Skylark Books is a registered trademark of Bantam Books, a division of
Random House, Inc. Registered in U.S. Patent and Trademark Office and in
other countries.

Copyright © 1999 by Lois Gladys Leppard
Cover illustration copyright © 1999 by Lori Earley

All rights reserved. No part of this book may be reproduced
or transmitted in any form or by any means, electronic
or mechanical, including photocopying, recording,
or by any information storage and retrieval system,
without permission in writing from the publisher.

If you purchased this book without a cover you should be aware that this
book is stolen property. It was reported as "unsold and destroyed" to the
publisher, and neither the author nor the publisher has received any payment
for this "stripped book."

ISBN 0-553-48659-4

Published simultaneously in the United States and Canada.

Bantam Books are published by Bantam Books, a division
of Random House, Inc. Its trademark, consisting of the words
"Bantam Books" and the portrayal of a rooster,
is Registered in U.S. Patent and Trademark Office
and in other countries. Marca Registrada.
Bantam Books 1540 Broadway, New York, New York 10036.

PRINTED IN THE UNITED STATES OF AMERICA

10 9 8 7 6 5 4 3 2 1

1

The Mystery Begins

"AMANDA ELIZABETH SHAW, will you please hurry up? I'd like to get home sometime before dark," Joe teased. He stood at the schoolhouse doorway waiting.

"Joe Woodard, if you call me all that mouthful again, I'll—I'll just walk home by myself," Mandie replied. "All my friends call me Mandie." She hastily tied on her bonnet and slipped into her lightweight coat, then reached to pick up her books from her desk.

Mr. Tallant, the schoolmaster of the one-room country schoolhouse, glanced at the two from his desk. "I appreciate y'all staying to help me straighten up, but you need to get going. It does get dark early now that fall has come."

"We're on our way. Good night, Mr. Tallant," Mandie said, tucking a stray lock of golden blond hair under her bonnet. She crossed the huge room to the door.

"Good night," Joe said. "We will see you bright and early tomorrow morning, since this is just Wednesday and we've got two more days to go before that lazy day called Saturday gets here."

The schoolmaster smiled as they left the schoolroom.

Mandie stepped outside onto the front porch of the log schoolhouse. The sun was already setting behind the tall chestnut trees down the road. She squinted her blue eyes, trying to see how much farther the sun had to go before it would actually drop out of sight over the mountain ahead. Darkness came early to Charley Gap, North Carolina, nestled in the shadow of the huge Nantahala Mountains.

Joe brushed past her down the steps. "Come on, slowpoke," he teased.

"I'm not as slow as you," Mandie said, rushing past him down the long lane toward the main road. She stopped to look back.

"We don't have to walk *that* fast, do we?" Joe

asked. He caught up with her and reached to take her books. "Are you going to let me carry these, or are you put out with me?"

Mandie gave him her books. "No, Joe, I'm not put out with you. I was just thinking about wintertime coming. Thanksgiving and Christmas will soon be here and 1897 will be gone."

"And we'll have a brand-new year," Joe added as they walked on.

"Only two years until we get a brand-new century." She sighed. "I wonder how it will feel."

Joe looked down at her. He was tall and thin for his eleven years. Mandie was short and small and two years younger.

"I don't believe it will feel any different from what this year does," he said with a serious look on his face. "Except that we will both be older."

"When are the McGoochins coming to see y'all?" Mandie asked.

"Friday night, I think," Joe replied. "My mother said—"

"Listen!" Mandie interrupted, stopping abruptly. "A horse is running away!"

Joe paused, and they listened to the crunching sound of rapidly moving wheels and a horse's hooves on the main road. "Whoever it is came to an awfully quick stop," he said.

Mandie hurried forward, and Joe followed. She couldn't see the road ahead, but she heard a man's voice call out, "Git there! Git!" Then the vehicle moved on.

Mandie and Joe ran to the end of the lane. A horse and buggy were racing down the road.

Mandie frowned. "I wonder why that buggy stopped. Do you think they lost something and stopped to look for it?"

"Whoever it was threw something out of the buggy. Maybe an animal of some kind," Joe said.

"Oh, no!" Mandie exclaimed. "Let's see if we can find whatever it was." She quickly walked off into the underbrush along the main road and began searching.

Joe stayed where he was. "Mandie, come on. We've got to go home. We're late already," he called after her.

"Wait till I look around just a little bit,"

Mandie answered, pushing back the bushes and peering beneath them.

"Mandie, come on!" Joe called impatiently.

"In a minute!" Mandie yelled back. She moved deeper into the bushes, taking care not to tear her coat on the branches.

"Mandie!" Joe yelled again. "If you don't come back here this minute I'm going on home without you."

"But, Joe—" Mandie started.

"Mandie, I mean it!" Joe interrupted. He bent forward to look for her. "Come on!"

"Just one more minute," Mandie said, pushing aside some branches. "There must be something somewhere."

"All right, I told you. I am going home, right now!" Joe said loudly. He turned to go on down the road. "Goodbye!"

Realizing that he really was leaving her, she scampered through the bushes. "Wait! I'm coming!" she yelled as she ran.

"Hurry up!" Joe called to her.

"I just wanted to see what that man threw out of the buggy," Mandie said between breaths as she caught up. "It wouldn't have taken long to search the whole side of the road back there."

"You can look tomorrow. We'll have more time," Joe told her as they walked on down the road.

"But whatever it was may be gone by then," Mandie protested. "Besides, my sister will be with us tomorrow. She's always in a hurry."

"Irene went on home ahead of us today, and she can do the same thing tomorrow if she doesn't want to help you look," Joe replied.

"If only I could have looked for a few more minutes," Mandie said, scuffing her high-top button-up shoes in the dirt. She knew Joe was right, but still, she might have found something.

"Well, I have to get home. I've got to help my mother get things ready for our company this weekend. Dad is expecting to make sick calls the rest of this week with all the flu and colds going around now."

Joe's father was the local doctor.

"Do you like your father being a doctor?" Mandie asked.

Joe shrugged. "He has been a doctor since before I was born. I suppose I'm used to having him take off in the middle of a meal to see a patient, or being gone overnight out into the country," he told her.

"Is Mr. McGoochin a doctor?" Mandie asked. She had to take big steps to keep up with Joe's long legs.

"No, but I wish he was so my dad wouldn't have to travel all over Swain County and into Macon County sometimes. The McGoochins live in Macon County. Mr. McGoochin has a huge farm over there," Joe said.

"Bigger than my father's hundred and twenty acres?" Mandie asked, trying to imagine a farm that large.

"Probably twice as large as your father's," Joe replied.

"Do they have any children?"

"A girl, Lucinda, who's a little younger than I am, and her brother, Michael, not quite as old as you," Joe said.

"Is Lucinda pretty?" Mandie asked, curious.

"I don't know. She's just an ordinary girl, I suppose," Joe said.

"Well, what does she look like?" Mandie pressed. "Does she have blond hair like mine?"

Joe reached down to yank Mandie's long plait. "Nobody has hair like yours."

Mandie pulled away from him as she walked on. "Joe, stop being silly."

"Then stop asking me silly questions. You'll see the McGoochins when y'all come over Friday night," he told her.

Mandie's family was invited over to visit. She hoped Lucinda and Michael were nice.

Joe walked faster.

Mandie paused to stamp her foot. "You go so fast I can't keep up with you," she protested. "My legs aren't as long as yours."

"Oh, I'm sorry, Mandie," Joe said. "My legs just got ahead of me."

Mandie walked on to catch up with him. "You don't have to walk all the way home with me, you know," she told him as they continued down the road.

"Oh, but I do," Joe replied. "I've been walking you home from school ever since the day you started."

"I'm not afraid to go by myself," Mandie told him. After all, she was nine years old.

"Suppose a panther came out of the woods. What would you do?"

Mandie looked up at him to see if he was teasing. He looked serious. "What would *you* do if a panther came across our path?" she asked.

"Wel-l-l-l . . ." Joe dragged the word out as he thought about the possibility. "Unless I had my rifle with me I'd try to outrun it, but those creatures are never seen this far down out of the mountain."

"So there's no reason for me to be afraid to walk home by myself," Mandie insisted.

But she secretly knew she didn't mean that. There were only sixteen pupils attending Mr. Tallant's school. Everyone except Mandie, her sister, Irene, and Joe lived in the opposite direction. The road home could be really lonely except for an occasional passing buggy or wagon. Even if Irene walked along with her she still wouldn't feel safe without Joe. However, she didn't want him to know that.

"Do you mean I'm walking two miles out of my way to see that you get home safe and sound and you don't think it's necessary?" Joe asked, glancing down at her.

Mandie saw the hurt look on his face. She couldn't stand that. "I'm sorry, Joe," she said. "I suppose I'm just all out of sorts because I keep wondering what that man threw out of that buggy. It might have been a hurt animal that needs our help." Her blue eyes looked directly into his brown ones.

"Oh, Mandie, you worry too much," Joe told her. "There will be other people passing by there. Someone will stop if need be."

"Mr. Tallant would help some poor animal, but since he lives in the schoolhouse building, I don't imagine he goes out every day," Mandie replied.

"Anyhow, you're almost home. I see your father working on that rail fence," Joe said as they approached the log cabin where Mandie lived.

Mandie's father had been splitting rails for days and had finally accumulated enough to begin the new fence around the Shaws' property.

"See you tomorrow," Joe told Mandie, handing her books over. He waved to Mr. Shaw and headed back down the road to his house.

"Goodbye," Mandie called as her father waved.

Mandie ran down to her father. He straightened up and put his arm around her. "And did my little blue-eyes learn something new today?" he asked, smoothing his curly red hair with his free hand.

"I learned there's no use arguing with Joe Woodard because he is going to get his way, no matter what," Mandie said, pouting as she looked up into her father's eyes. They were the same bright blue as hers.

"Have you been arguing with Joe?" Mr. Shaw asked as he released her and resumed his work on the fence.

"Not exactly," Mandie said. "But there was this buggy that stopped down near the schoolhouse . . ." She told him what had happened.

"Since you didn't actually see whoever it was, they might not have thrown anything out, Amanda," her father reminded her. "Anyway, Joe was right. You did need to get home before dark. Otherwise your mother and I would have been worried about you. Your sister has been home a long time."

"Didn't Irene tell you that Joe and I stayed to help Mr. Tallant straighten up the schoolroom?" Mandie asked.

"No, I saw her come down the road to the house, but I didn't talk to her," Mr. Shaw explained. "She went inside, and I haven't seen her since."

"She's probably down at the spring with that Tommy Lester," Mandie said. Lately Tommy was all Irene talked about. "That's where she always is when Mama sends me to find her."

"Do you have homework?" her father asked.

"Some," Mandie replied.

"Then you'd better get in the house and get it done. It won't be long till suppertime," he said. "And it won't be long before I have to quit and come inside. The sun has about disappeared for the day."

Mandie started on toward the house but then she turned back. "Joe thinks the new century will be just like this one, nothing different. What do you think, Daddy?"

"I see you two have been carrying on some serious conversation," he said. "Amanda, there is no way to foretell the future. We'll just have to wait and see what it brings. Not much any of us can do about it. Don't worry that pretty little head. Just enjoy what's left of *this* century."

Mandie frowned. "But, Daddy, it's all right to just think about it, isn't it? After all, we have to think about everything else."

"Of course," Mr. Shaw said. "Provided that's not all you think about. Right now go think about your homework and get that done."

Mandie hastened on toward the house. "Just a little bit of arithmetic," she mumbled to herself. "And memorize 'The Village Blacksmith,' a poem I already know, with every period and comma. I don't know why Mr. Tallant gave us such a favorite poem to learn when everybody already knows it." She paused for a moment. "But I'm not exactly sure who wrote it."

She continued down the lane. Maybe when the new century came in Mr. Tallant would give them something better to do. Right now she wanted to ask her mama what time they would go over to the Woodards' house on Friday night. And tomorrow morning she would search for whatever that man had thrown out of the buggy before school. Because she was sure there was something to find.

Mandie would be counting the minutes until she could investigate. This was the first mystery she had ever been involved in. She liked the idea of solving puzzles like this one.

2

Hurry Up and Wait

THE NEXT MORNING Mandie hurried through breakfast to be ready when Joe came by. Maybe he would come a little early, since he knew how eager she was to search for whatever had been thrown from the buggy.

"What's the rush?" Irene asked from the table. She was two years older than Mandie and thought she knew everything about everything. She pushed her long, dark hair behind her ear as she watched Mandie fill her lunch basket.

"I was just thinking Joe might come by early this morning," Mandie told her. "And I want to be ready. You'd better get a move on yourself."

"You're so fast. How about throwing something in my lunch basket while you're at it? Two of those sausage biscuits and two apples and—"

"Fix it yourself," Mandie interrupted her

bossy sister. "You have as much time as I do. Besides, if you aren't ready when Joe gets here you don't have to walk to school with us anyhow." She tucked a napkin over the contents of her basket and closed the little straw lid.

Mrs. Shaw came bustling into the kitchen. She wore long, full skirts, which made her look overweight, and she combed her dark hair into a bun on top of her head. "Aren't you finished yet, Irene? That school bell is not going to wait for you." She began stacking the dirty dishes on the table, her dark eyes watching the girls.

"Where's Daddy, Mama?" Mandie asked. She picked up her basket and started for the door. She didn't tell her mother about the buggy mystery. Unlike her father, who always listened to anything she had to say, her mother was always too busy.

"He's already gone out to the back line to bring more logs up to the house to split for the fence," her mother said, sliding between the chair where Irene was sitting and the wall as she moved around the table.

Irene finally stood up. "I'll catch up with you in a minute," she told Mandie, wiping her mouth. She hurriedly picked up her lunch basket from the sideboard and began filling it with food, two of everything.

Mandie stopped to watch. She knew her sister didn't eat all that food. Irene gave half of it to Tommy Lester, who never seemed to have enough to eat even though he brought a much larger basket to school with him every day.

"I'm going to get my coat and bonnet. I'll be out front until Joe gets here," Mandie told her.

Mandie hurried into the front room. Next to the ladder to the attic were pegs where the Shaws hung their coats. She and Irene slept upstairs on cornshuck mattresses. It certainly wasn't fancy, but it was the warmest room in the house because the heat from the big iron cookstove rose up there. Drawn curtains partitioned off her parents' bed in the front room.

Mandie set her basket on the little table by the ladder and quickly put on her coat and bonnet. She glanced in the mirror over the table to be sure all her hair was tucked in. Taking her gloves from her coat pocket, she left them on the table. It wasn't really cold enough yet to wear them.

"Wait for me!" Irene yelled as she came rushing into the room for her coat and hat.

Mandie picked up her books from the table and moved on toward the front door. "I'm going outside to wait for Joe," she told her. "You'd better hurry." She opened the door, closed it behind her, and stopped on the front porch to look up the road. Sure enough, there was Joe, hurrying down the lane from the main road. She ran to meet him.

"I was wishing you would get here early so I could search the bushes by the schoolhouse," Mandie told him, smiling as they met in the lane.

Joe reached for her books. "I know," he said. "I figured you wanted to do that."

The two turned to go on toward the road as Irene came running after them. "Wait for me!" she yelled again as her long legs quickly covered the distance between her and them.

The sky was clear, but the sun was being lazy about getting out of bed. The birds were singing and chirping. The squirrels were scampering about, hunting for breakfast.

When the three came within sight of the

schoolhouse Mandie slowed down. "I'd like to begin looking here."

Irene frowned. "For what?"

"Oh, something I was looking for yesterday," Mandie said, wanting to keep the mystery secret.

"Like what?" her sister asked.

"I'll let you know if I find it," Mandie replied.

"Well, I'm going on to school," Irene declared, walking down the road.

"Wait," Mandie said, holding out her lunch basket. "Will you take this for me?"

"I suppose so," Irene said with a grumble. She grabbed Mandie's basket and raced on down the road.

Joe carried his lunch in a leather pouch slung over his shoulder along with the strap that held his books together. "I could have put that with mine," he said.

At that moment Mandie heard a faint meow. "Did you hear that?" she asked in a loud whisper as she bent to look through the bushes along the road.

"What?" Joe asked, and then, as the sound was repeated, he nodded. "I heard it. Just sounded like a cat, that's all."

"Kitty, kitty!" Mandie called out as she moved into the bushes.

"Do you see anything?" Joe asked, lifting a branch.

"Not yet," Mandie replied. "Kitty, kitty! Where are you?"

The underbrush was dry and brittle. Mandie carefully pulled away from the briars to keep from getting stuck. The cat had not made any more noise, and she couldn't figure out which way it had gone.

"We'll be late for school," Joe said impatiently.

At that moment Mandie heard a faint meow from deeper in the bushes. "Just a minute!" she called back, pushing her way forward.

"Mandie!" Joe yelled. "Being late will cost us a grade in deportment. Can't you look for that cat after school?"

"I need to see if the cat is all right," Mandie called back.

"Well, I'm leaving," Joe said. He started walking down the road.

Mandie saw him through the bushes and

quickly made her way out. "Wait, I'm coming," she said.

Joe frowned as she caught up with him. "Do you realize what a mess you are? You've got briars all over your coat and a snag in your bonnet," he said.

Mandie felt her bonnet. "I hope it's not bad or Mama won't like it at all," she said. She couldn't find any rips—and she didn't have time to remove the bonnet and examine it.

As they neared the schoolhouse Mandie saw Rodney Jones, one of the older students, standing beneath the bell in the tower. "Run!" she cried as she picked up her long skirts and raced for the schoolhouse door.

Joe quickly followed, and the two rushed breathlessly into the schoolroom, removing their coats as they went and tossing them onto pegs by the doorway. Just as they both flopped down at their desks, Rodney began pulling the rope and the old iron bell gave notice that school was in session.

Mr. Tallant rose behind his desk at the far side of the room and greeted the pupils. "Good morning," he said, glancing at each corner of the room. The sixteen boys and girls were grouped according to grade level. Mandie didn't sit in the same section with Joe, since he was two years older. Somehow, though, Joe managed to pass notes to Mandie now and then. She loved his notes. They were usually written in poetry.

"Good morning," the pupils chorused back.

"We will rise now, face the flag, and pledge our allegiance," Mr. Tallant told them. Everyone stood with their hands over their hearts as he led the recitation.

"You may be seated now," Mr. Tallant said after the pledge. He looked at the papers on his desk. "This morning Group One will draw a picture of the flag. Group Two will stand and recite the poem I assigned yesterday, 'The Village Blacksmith.' Group Three will do problems one through three in chapter three of your arithmetic book. And, finally, Group Four will study its history lesson in preparation for an examination tomorrow." He looked around the room. "Any questions?"

No one spoke. Mandie's group, Group Two,

would be reciting the poem. Suddenly she could not remember who wrote it. She had looked it up last night, but now the poet's name escaped her.

"Amanda Shaw, you will begin the recitation. Please stand," Mr. Tallant said.

Mandie stood up. " 'The Village Blacksmith,' " she said, and quickly sailed right through the poem without any mistakes. She hoped Mr. Tallant would not notice that she had not identified the poet. And evidently he did not. She quickly sat down and listened to Esther Rogan, who was next. " 'The Village Blacksmith,' by Henry W. Longfellow," Esther began, and continued to the end.

Henry W. Longfellow. That was it.

While the other two pupils were reciting the poem, Mandie's mind wandered. She thought about the cat crying in the bushes. Was that what someone had thrown out of the buggy? If so, why would anyone desert a poor animal like that? Maybe she could catch it and take it home with her. But her mother was not especially fond of cats. Then Mandie brightened. Her father usually went along with anything she did. He did like cats. Maybe he would be willing to take in a stray.

The morning passed pretty quickly, and soon it was time for the noon break. No one was allowed to leave the school grounds during recess, so Mandie had to be content to sit at a table under the fall-colored trees with Joe.

"I'll be glad when school is out for the day so I can go look for that cat," Mandie told Joe between bites of her sausage biscuit.

He bit into his ham biscuit. "But what if the cat is wild? It might try to scratch or bite you."

"Not if I'm not mean to it," Mandie objected. "Anyway, whether the cat came from that buggy or not, it's lost or doesn't have a home. I think it would be glad for me to take it in."

Mandie swallowed the last of her biscuit. "If I give it something to eat, it will understand that I will be good to it. Don't you think?"

"I suppose so. Cats and dogs are usually agreeable with whoever feeds them," Joe conceded. "But the problem is catching it."

Mandie nodded. That could take some time.

"Irene could go ahead home and tell Mama what we are doing," she said. But that might make matters worse. Her mother wouldn't want her bringing a stray cat home. "I'll ask Irene to tell my father," Mandie decided. "He'll understand."

So that's what Mandie did. After school she told her sister she'd be late getting home and why. "Would you please tell Daddy what I'm doing?" she asked.

Irene looked down at her younger sister. "You don't want me to tell Mama?"

"No, I'd rather tell her myself," Mandie said.

Irene shrugged her thin shoulders. "All right, as long as you do tell Mama when you get home."

"I will," Mandie promised. "Thanks, Irene."

As Irene went on up the road toward home, Mandie and Joe stopped near the place where they had heard the cat. Mandie began searching the bushes while Joe kept watch on the road in case the cat ran out.

Mandie tried to move softly so that the cat wouldn't be scared away. She carefully pushed back limbs in the underbrush, scanning the ground. Suddenly she heard a loud meow right behind her. Quickly turning, she saw the animal at last. It was a large black-and-white spotted cat, and it was sitting there looking up at her. She slowly reached down to pick it up.

"Come on, kitty. I won't hurt you," she said softly as she managed to lift the heavy animal.

The cat wriggled in her arms as though it wanted to get down, but when Mandie began rubbing the fur on its head it became still and began to purr. Mandie carefully worked her way back through the bushes and came out on the road where Joe was watching.

"You found it!" Joe said.

"Yes, and I'm going to take it home with me," Mandie said, holding the animal tight. The cat's fur felt soft and warm in her hands.

"I don't know if that's a good idea," Joe said slowly.

"Why?"

"That cat is tame," Joe pointed out. "It must belong to somebody. And if you take it home with you, its owner will never find it."

Mandie frowned as she thought about this.

"Well, if it belongs to someone, why is it here in the woods?"

"Cats run off sometimes," Joe said. "Maybe it was chasing a squirrel or a rabbit and ended up far away from its home. I'm sure it must belong to somebody. It's not a wild stray cat. You can tell that."

"But it's been here since we heard it yesterday, and it's probably hungry and tired," Mandie objected as she continued petting the cat in her arms.

"And if you put it back down it will find its way home sooner or later," Joe insisted. "If you take that cat home and it does belong to someone, that will be stealing."

Mandie bit her lip and slowly put the cat down. "No, I couldn't steal anything," she said regretfully as the cat rubbed around her ankles. "It doesn't look exactly well. Maybe it's sick. Maybe that's why it's crying so much."

Joe nodded. "It looks tired."

Mandie had an idea. "If it's still here tomorrow after school, do you think it would be all right for me to take it home? It would be awfully hungry by then."

"Tomorrow's Friday, the last day of school this week. If it's still here I will help you catch it. Now, come on. We've got to walk fast so we won't be too late."

Mandie smiled up at him as they started on down the road. She knew she could count on Joe.

"Meow."

Mandie turned around. The cat was following them. She stopped and touched Joe's arm. "Look, it's coming with us anyway!" she said.

Joe shooed the cat. "Go home now, kitty," he said.

But the cat just stopped and looked at him and then at Mandie. It circled Joe and moved close to Mandie's legs.

Mandie stooped down. "You have to go home, wherever you belong, kitty. I'll take you home with me tomorrow if you're still here."

The cat meowed sadly. Then it began rubbing around Mandie's ankles as she straightened up.

"Come on. Let's walk fast. Maybe it'll get discouraged and go on back wherever it came from," Joe told her.

With a disappointed sigh, Mandie hurried along beside Joe down the road. Every time she looked back, the cat was still following them.

"Don't pay any attention to it so it'll just go away," Joe told her.

"I don't think it's going to go away," Mandie replied as they hastened on.

And she was right. The cat was still behind them when they came to the lane leading to Mandie's house. Mandie stooped down and picked up the cat, which immediately began purring. "Well, it followed us home anyway. I'm going to at least feed it," she said, defiantly looking up at Joe.

Joe laughed. "All right. I know that's exactly what you wanted to happen, but don't be surprised if someone comes looking for their cat."

"For the time being I'm going to claim it," Mandie said as Joe handed her her books.

"See you in the morning," he called back to her as he rushed on down the road.

Mandie spied her father working on the fence. No one else was in sight. Juggling the cat under one arm and her books under the other, she rushed to drop her books on the front porch and then ran across the field to her father. He looked up as he saw her.

"Now what have you got there?" he asked.

"Oh, it's this poor cat that I found on the road near the schoolhouse," Mandie began. "And it has been in the woods for at least two days and it followed me home." She planted a kiss on the cat's head. "Daddy, may I keep it? May I? May I? I've never had a pet all my own before."

Mr. Shaw laughed. "I suppose you may keep it until someone comes along and claims it. However, I don't think you'd better take it into the house. You know your mother does not exactly like cats. You could make it a bed in the barn and take food and water to it."

"Oh, thank you, Daddy," Mandie said excitedly. "I'll go do that right now. Thank you!" She ran back across the field toward the barn.

Inside the barn she set the cat down. "Now, you stay right here and I'll go get you something to eat, you hear?"

The cat purred as it looked up at Mandie. When she started to leave the barn, it ran after her.

"No, no, you can't go in the house," Mandie said. She looked around the inside of the barn. Where could she leave it so that it couldn't get out and follow her? She spied a deserted chicken coop over in one corner. It was quite large and would have plenty of room for the cat to walk around inside. Picking up the cat, she ran over, opened the door, and pushed the cat inside. The cat immediately began clawing to get out.

Mandie put her hands on her hips.

"I'm sorry, but you have to stay there until you get used to being in the barn. You absolutely can't follow me into the house. Now, I'll be right back with something for you to eat." Mandie bent down and shook her forefinger at the cat. "Now, don't make too much noise. I'll be right back, you hear?"

Gathering up her skirt, she quickly ran to the house. She hoped she would not see her mother, because then she would have to explain why she was taking food out of the house. *A cat all my own,* she thought happily. Even though it might be for a short time, a few days were better than none. Then again, maybe the owner would never show up and the cat would be all hers!

3

Hoping

MANDIE SOFTLY OPENED the back door and entered the kitchen. There was no one there. The house seemed awfully quiet. She looked into the front room, which was the parlor. "Mama! Mama!"

There was no answer. She walked through the room to the front door and retrieved her books, which she had left on the porch.

"I wonder where Mama and Irene are," she murmured as she came back inside and placed her books on the table by the ladder.

Mandie hurried back into the kitchen and opened the warmer on the big iron cookstove. Her mother kept leftovers in there. Today Mandie found a sausage biscuit. Closing the door of the warmer, she picked up a chipped bowl from under the dry sink and filled it with water from the pail on the shelf.

At that moment her mother came in through the back door.

"Amanda, take off your bonnet and coat and get in there and do your homework," Mrs. Shaw told her as she laid a slab of ham on the worktable beside the stove. "We need to straighten up the smokehouse while you girls are out of school this weekend. I had to sort through a mess to find this ham here."

Mandie paused with the biscuit and bowl of water in her hands. "I have to feed the cat, Mama. I'll be right back." She started toward the door.

"Cat? What cat?" her mother asked as she reached for a large butcher knife to carve off a hunk of the ham for cooking.

"I found a homeless cat in the woods near the schoolhouse and it followed me home. It was crying and crying and seemed to be hungry," Mandie carefully explained.

Mrs. Shaw laid her knife down. "Now, you know I don't like cats, and I won't have you bringing one around here. You'll have to take it right back where you found it."

Mandie swallowed. "But, Mama, I showed it to Daddy and he said I could keep it in the barn until someone comes to claim it. Please let me keep it. I won't let it come in the house," Mandie pleaded.

"Your daddy said you could keep it?" Mrs. Shaw questioned her.

"Yes, ma'am," Mandie replied. "He said the cat must belong to someone and that they would come and get it when they found out where it was. Please, Mama."

Her mother sighed. "Well, if your daddy said you could keep it . . ." Mrs. Shaw began cutting the ham. "But I won't have it in this house. Now, you remember that."

"Thank you, Mama," Mandie said, a big smile breaking across her face. "I'll go feed it, and I'll be right back to do my homework."

Holding the bowl of water in one hand and the biscuit in the other, Mandie hurried outside to the barn.

The cat was meowing loudly as it scratched around in the chicken coop.

"I brought you something to eat. Look here," Mandie said, crouching down to open the chicken coop door. She laid the biscuit on the straw inside and set the bowl of water in a corner.

The cat smelled the biscuit. To Mandie's surprise, it backed off, meowing loudly as it looked up at Mandie.

"Come on and eat. I know you must be hungry," Mandie said, moving the biscuit in front of the cat. Again the animal stepped away from it, and continued to cry.

"Oh, goodness, you must not like sausage," Mandie said, frowning. She closed the door of the coop and stood up. "I'm sorry, but that's all I could find to eat right now. If you don't want that, you'll just have to wait until Mama cooks the ham for supper." She reached through the coop and stroked the cat's paw. "I have to go now, but I'll be back."

As Mandie left the barn, she could hear the cat meowing and scratching around in the chicken coop, trying to get out. Suddenly another idea dawned on Mandie. Maybe the cat was sick. It did seem to cry an awful lot. Maybe

Joe's father, Dr. Woodard, would come and look at it. She would ask him when she and her family went visiting tomorrow.

She skipped on down the lane to the back door, quickly removing her bonnet and coat as she entered the kitchen. She stopped by the cookstove, where her mother was sliding a pan holding the ham into the oven.

Mrs. Shaw straightened up to look at her. "Get that homework done now," she said.

"Mama, I was just wondering what time we're going over to the Woodards' house tomorrow night," Mandie said.

"We're going to eat over there, so we'll probably have to leave as soon as you and Irene get home from school."

"All right, Mama. I'll come straight home," Mandie promised. She went into the front room to hang her coat and bonnet on the pegs by the ladder. Then she picked up her books and settled down in a chair by the window.

Mandie was so thrilled about owning a cat that it was hard for her to concentrate on her lessons. The cat was the most wonderful thing that had ever happened to her! She just hoped it was not sick.

"Two times two equals four, plus six equals ten, and then divided by five equals two. Just what I started off with." Mandie thought aloud as she did her arithmetic, which was her favorite subject. Figuring out numbers was like solving a mystery, and she knew she was pretty good at playing detective.

"I see you found that stray cat," Irene said, strolling into the room. "It's out there in the barn howling its head off."

"I know. Maybe when I feed it after supper it will hush," Mandie said with a sigh as she looked up from her book.

"That cat wants out of that chicken coop. That's what's wrong with it," Irene replied. She sat down across the room with her books.

"Do you think so?" Mandie asked.

"Of course," Irene said.

"But it was crying like that when I found it, before I put it in the chicken coop," Mandie said.

"Mandie, cats are not supposed to be shut up

like chickens. They are supposed to be allowed to roam around. Why have you got it in that pen anyway?" Irene asked.

"You know Mama doesn't like cats, so I had to be sure it wouldn't come into the house," Mandie said. "How else could I keep it out?"

"By keeping the back door of the house closed," Irene said. "Believe me, I know what I'm talking about. You just let that cat out of that chicken coop and it will hush up."

"Suppose it runs away?" Mandie asked.

"If it does, it's probably looking for its owner and you shouldn't keep it from finding its own home anyway," Irene said. "How would you like it if you got lost and someone shut you up so you couldn't go home?"

"I suppose I could let it out just in case it wanted to go home." Mandie said thoughtfully. "But maybe if I feed it real good it won't want to go back wherever it came from. I'm pretty sure it was thrown out of that buggy. I don't believe it really has a home."

"Who would throw a cat out of a buggy, Mandie?" Irene asked, opening her notebook.

"Now I have to get this homework done. Don't talk to me."

"Mine is almost finished, so as soon as I get done I'll go help Mama set the table. You can help clean up after we eat then," Mandie said, quickly jotting down figures.

"All right, all right, just don't talk to me. I'm trying to learn my spelling," Irene said. She bent closer to her spelling book and frowned at the words.

Mandie finished her lesson, closed her book, and put everything back on the table by the ladder where it would all be ready for school the next morning. Then she went to the kitchen to help her mother.

Mrs. Shaw wiped off the big table with a dishrag. "Now you can get the dishes."

Mandie loved setting the table. It was like playing a game. She put every piece in the exact proper place. Their utensils and dishes were just a plain everyday kind, but she pretended they were real silverware and china like Miss Abigail's. Miss Abigail was a very wealthy lady. The entire school had once been invited to her house for a surprise birthday party for Mr. Tallant, their schoolteacher. Mandie had decided then that she would someday own things like Miss Abigail's shiny silver teapot and all those forks, spoons, and knives to match it. While at Miss Abigail's, she'd discovered that the dainty china cups and plates would actually make a little ringing sound if she accidentally struck them with the silverware. She observed every detail and began practicing at home. Her mother had allowed her to cut up a white bedsheet and make napkins out of it and had shown her how to roll and whip the edges, just like the edges of Miss Abigail's linen ones.

Mr. Shaw came in through the back door and smiled as he watched Mandie. "I see we're eating in style tonight," he teased.

"She gets it from you, Jim," Mrs. Shaw remarked. She stood at the stove, stirring a pot of beans.

"Oh, Daddy, doesn't it look nice?" Mandie asked as she stepped back to view the table.

"Absolutely," he agreed. He picked up the pail of water from the dry sink and poured some into a washpan. "What did you do with that cat?" he asked as he washed his face.

"I put it in the barn like you told me to," Mandie replied. "But, you know, it sure doesn't like being in that chicken coop."

"Chicken coop? You shut that cat up in a chicken coop?" he asked as he dried his face on a towel.

"Amanda, cats can't live in chicken coops," her mother said.

"But you both told me to keep it out of the house. How else am I going to do that?" Mandie asked, frowning.

"You have to let it out of that coop," her father said. "You'll just have to keep the back door closed."

"That's what Irene said, too," Mandie said.

"And Irene was right," her mother told her as she opened the oven to check on the biscuits baking inside. "That back door is supposed to be kept closed all the time anyhow, what with chickens roaming about the yard, and flies and mosquitoes, not to mention the dust and the wind."

"Well, all right then," Mandie said, shrugging her small shoulders. "When I feed it after supper I'll let it out."

"Get one of those old crates in the barn and fill it with straw, and get an old piece of cloth to cover it," her father said. "Then you'll have a bed for it."

"But where do I put the box?" Mandie asked. "I've never had a cat before."

Mr. Shaw reached down to pat Mandie's head. "I know," he said. "It takes time to learn all these things. Just put the box in a corner."

"I'll give you an old towel I was going to use for a dishrag," Mrs. Shaw said as she pulled the pan of biscuits out of the oven. "Now, run get your sister. It's time to eat."

"Here I am," Irene said as she came into the kitchen. Looking at Mandie, she said, "I told you that cat couldn't stay shut up in the chicken coop."

"We've had enough said about that cat. Let's sit down and eat," Mrs. Shaw said. She spooned a bowl full of beans and took it to the table. Then she put the biscuits on a plate and the ham on a platter and set them next to the beans.

"Amanda, get the beets over there, and, Irene, you bring the onions."

"I'll pour the coffee," Mr. Shaw said as he reached for two cups and saucers in the cabinet. He filled them with coffee from the pot on the stove.

"Hot cocoa for you girls," Mrs. Shaw said. She poured the steaming liquid from another pot on the stove into two cups.

"Mmm," Mandie said. She loved hot cocoa.

With everyone helping, they soon got everything on the table and sat down to eat. The girls waited for their father to give thanks and then began filling their plates.

"Do we get dressed up to go to Joe's house tomorrow night?" Irene asked.

"No, but you girls will certainly have to hurry home and change into clean clothes. I never have figured out what y'all do in that schoolhouse that gets you so mussed up," Mrs. Shaw told her.

"Oh, Mama, it's just a little ink now and then and sometimes a little dirt from playing at recess," Irene said, quickly eating her beans.

"And chalk," Mandie added. "That shows up something awful on dark dresses. I try to wipe it off."

"I'll put on my red calico," Irene said.

"And I'll wear my blue gingham," Mandie decided.

"I've been thinking," Mrs. Shaw said. "You girls are going to have to have some new clothes for the winter because you've both outgrown everything that's warm." She turned to her husband. "I'll have to go down to Bradshaw's store and get some material to make them a dress or two apiece." She sipped her coffee.

"Get whatever you need," Mr. Shaw said, cutting the ham on his plate.

"Can I go with you, Mama, so I can pick out what I want?" Irene asked eagerly. She held her fork in midair as she waited for the answer.

"No, no, you are not going with me. You'll be trying to get me to buy everything in that store," Mrs. Shaw told her.

"Mama, could I have a tam like Irene's? I'm too old to wear a bonnet," Mandie begged.

"Other girls your age wear bonnets," Irene protested.

"They don't. Not all of them," Mandie replied.

"You girls finish your supper. No more discussion now. I'll buy whatever I think you need and whatever we can afford," Mrs. Shaw told them.

Mandie chewed her meat. "I have to hurry anyhow so that poor cat can have some supper."

"And I will go with you and help you make a bed. It's already dark out there, and I don't want you carrying a lantern," Mr. Shaw said.

Mandie looked across to the room's only window. The curtain was still open, but the light from the lamp on the small table in front of it reflected on the glass and she couldn't see much outside. Her mother always lit the lamp in the kitchen when she began the evening meal.

When the meal was finished Mandie took food scraps from the table for the cat and got her coat and bonnet. Her father lit the lantern and walked with her to the barn. He was right. It was almost completely dark.

As they entered the building, Mr. Shaw flashed the lantern toward the chicken coop, where the cat was still meowing. "You go on over there and feed it and I'll find a box and we'll make a bed."

Mandie hurried to open the door of the coop and put the plate of food in front of the cat. "Here's your supper, just like I promised," she said soothingly.

But the cat wasn't interested in the food. As soon as Mandie got the door open it slipped past her—and ran out of the barn!

"Come back here!" Mandie called as she started to rush after it.

"Let it go," her father told her as he brought a box over near the coop and set it down. "It'll come back for the food after we leave."

Mandie stopped. "Do you really think it will?"

"It must be pretty hungry. It will come back. It just wanted to be sure you didn't shut it up in that coop again," he said. "Now let's get a little straw and line this box."

Mandie could hear their horse, Dangit, moving about in his stall, and the cow, Susie, in the next one. She followed her father across the barn. "Maybe that cat heard the horse and the cow and was afraid of them," she suggested as she helped him get straw from the pile and carried it to the box.

"I don't think so," Mr. Shaw said. "Cats seem to know they can outrun large animals like that."

"I sure hope it comes back after all the trouble I've gone through for it," Mandie said, tucking a stray piece of hair under her bonnet. "Besides, it's nice to own a real live cat."

"Don't count on owning it too much," her father reminded her. "Like I told you, it probably belongs to someone, and they may come and get it."

"I know, but I hope they won't," Mandie said. "Oh, shucks! I just remembered. I forgot to get that old towel from Mama."

"I found something that will work," Mr. Shaw said, pulling down a large rag from a nearby nail and placing it on the box. "There."

"Thanks, Daddy," Mandie said, smiling up at her father. "Thanks for letting me keep the cat."

And she desperately hoped she would be able to keep it and no one would claim it.

4

Visitors

MANDIE WOKE THE next morning to the sound of birds twittering outside her window. The sun was peeping over the mountain, lightening the sky with a faint yellow tint. The day was going to be clear and sunshiny.

"The cat," Mandie murmured to herself as she remembered how the cat had wandered off when she had let it out of the chicken coop. Maybe it had come back overnight. Oh, how she hoped it had. She would just creep out of bed, down the ladder, and out the back door to see.

Quietly putting on her clothes so as not to wake Irene, she sniffed the air to see if her father was up. She could always tell by the aroma of coffee perking whether he was in the kitchen or not. No scent this morning, but she figured it wouldn't be long before he was making a pot of coffee. Grabbing an old hooded cloak hanging from a peg in her attic room, Mandie hurriedly slipped into it and softly descended the ladder.

She knew the back door creaked at a certain point when it was opened. She slowly pulled it just wide enough for her to slip through and then eased it shut behind her.

The morning air felt warm for the season, and Mandie pushed back her hood as she ran toward the barn. She slowed down at the doorway—she didn't want to startle the cat—and peered inside. The early light was still dim in the barn. She figured the cat would be meowing its heart out if it was in the barn. To her dismay, though, there was no sound other than those made by the cow and the horse moving around in their stalls.

Creeping over to the chicken coop, Mandie checked the food and water she had left the night before. Nothing had been touched. She sighed with disappointment.

Walking around inside the barn, she called, "Kitty, kitty, come here, kitty."

The only response she got was from Dangit, snorting as he moved restlessly in his stall. Then suddenly Susie mooed loudly. Mandie jumped at the sound.

"Oh, shucks!" Mandie exclaimed as she stamped her foot. "You two animals will scare off the cat if it's anywhere near here." But the horse and the cow kept up their noise.

Mandie quickly searched the barn, but there was no sign of the cat. She went outside to look around the yard and saw her father coming toward her. She ran to meet him.

"Daddy, that cat didn't come back!" she exclaimed. "I've looked everywhere. It didn't even eat the food I left for it. Do you think it still might come back? Do you?" She turned to walk with him back to the barn.

Mr. Shaw smiled as he looked down at his small blond daughter. "If you want to keep that cat, then I hope it comes back. I would suggest you look for it on your way to school this morning. You said you found it on the road up there. Maybe it went back that way."

"I will, Daddy," Mandie told him as they entered the barn. "But when I found it on the road it seemed to be lost."

"I've got to let old Dangit out to pasture right now," her father said, going to open the door to the horse's stall.

Dangit snorted, quickly rubbed his nose on Mr. Shaw's shoulder, and then bounded out of the barn through the back door, which opened into the pasture.

Mandie watched thoughtfully. "Do you think that cat could ever learn the routine of things like Dangit has?"

"I suppose so if you taught it," her father said, closing the door behind the horse. "Now I've got to get back before that coffee all perks away." He started up the pathway to the house.

"Aren't you going to let Susie out this morning?" Mandie asked, following him.

"Not until she's milked. I just happened to get up earlier than usual this morning. I thought I heard someone in the kitchen," Mr. Shaw said, grinning at his daughter.

"I really and truly tried to be quiet when I got up. I even listened for the creak in the back door so it would go real slowlike and not so loud," Mandie said.

"I was already awake anyhow and thought I'd check on the cat for you, but you beat me to it," Mr. Shaw said.

"I hope it comes back," Mandie said.

As they reached the back door of the house, Mr. Shaw paused with his hand on the knob and looked down at Mandie. "Since we're both up so bright and early, what do you say we cook breakfast and surprise your mother when she gets up?"

Mandie grinned. "Oh, yes, let's do." She loved doing chores with her father.

Inside the kitchen the two quickly removed their wraps and began preparations for the morning meal. Mr. Shaw poured himself a cup of coffee from the pot and measured out the flour for the biscuits. Mandie put on a pot of water to boil and brought the can of grits from the pantry.

"We'll have ham with our grits this morning," her father told her. "Your mother put what was left from last night in the warmer. We could scramble up a few eggs to go with it."

"I'll get them," Mandie told him as she opened the door of the huge pie safe. Inside sat a large bowl of eggs, nestled in salt to keep them fresh. Mandie carefully took out half a dozen and put them in a bowl. Then she went over near the stove where the pots and pans hung on wallhooks. Stepping up on the woodbox, she managed to get down a large iron frying pan.

"You should have waited for me to reach that for you," her father said, his hands covered with flour as he rolled out the dough for biscuits.

"I got it down all right," Mandie said, placing the frying pan on one of the caps of the big iron cookstove.

While Mandie melted butter in the pan for the eggs, Mr. Shaw cut out the biscuits with the biscuit cutter and lifted them onto a large baking sheet.

Mandie enjoyed cooking, especially with her father. There was nothing she loved better than helping her father. She loved him so much, and she could feel his love for her when he looked at her and smiled.

When everything was within five minutes of being done, Mrs. Shaw came into the kitchen.

"My, my! I should sleep late more often," she said, smiling. "The only bad thing is I know you two always dirty up every pot and pan in the house—and then I usually end up washing them."

"It's quicker that way," Mr. Shaw replied, laughing as he checked on the biscuits in the oven. "Is Irene up? Everything's about ready."

"I'll see," Mrs. Shaw said, hurrying back out of the room.

When she returned, Irene was with her and everything was on the table. Mandie surveyed their work with pride. Irene never would have done all this. She wasn't interested in anything much except Tommy Lester. Mandie had never seen anything special about Tommy.

They sat down and began breakfast. Although she was worried that the cat would never come back, Mandie enjoyed her food. Somehow it just tasted better when she and her father prepared it.

Since they ate a little earlier than usual Mandie had time afterward to search the barn again for the cat. But there was no sign of it.

The girls got ready to leave for school and picked up their lunch baskets. Their mother reminded them, "No fooling around after school now. Remember we are going to the Woodards' as soon as y'all get home. And, Amanda, there'll be no time to search for that cat, either. If it wants to come back it will. Now, get going."

"Yes, ma'am," Mandie said as she hurried out the front door.

"Yes, Mama," Irene called back as she raced after Mandie, who was running to meet Joe at the road.

During school that day Mandie couldn't keep her mind on the lessons. Where had the cat gone? Would it come back?

By the time Mandie and Irene came home from school and changed their clothes, Mr. Shaw had the wagon waiting in the lane by the front porch. Mandie kept trying to look around the yard, upset because she didn't have time to run out to the barn to see if the cat had come back. She would much rather have stayed home just in case the cat returned than go to the Woodards' and meet those strangers.

However, when Mr. Shaw pulled the wagon into the Woodards' driveway, Mandie changed her mind. Joe was sitting in the yard swing with a very pretty girl dressed in the latest style of coat and tam. Mandie put her hand up to her old bonnet. She hated it. She was too old to wear a bonnet.

Dr. Woodard came out into the yard. "Hello there," he said, welcoming them.

As they stepped down from the wagon, Mr. Miller walked over. He lived and worked on the Woodards' farm. "I'll take care of the horse," he said, taking the reins.

"Come in the house," Dr. Woodard was saying to the Shaws when a buggy rolled up. It was Mr. Tallant, their schoolteacher.

"Alight and come in," Dr. Woodard called to him. "Leave the buggy there. Mr. Miller will take care of it." The adults all went into the house.

Joe smiled at Mandie and Irene. "Y'all come sit down with us." He moved to one end of the long swing.

"No, I think I'll just take a walk," Irene said, starting down the lane.

"If you do you'll miss Tommy Lester," Joe told her with a teasing grin.

Irene instantly stopped and looked back. "He didn't tell me he was coming," she said.

"That's because he didn't know about it until this afternoon. His parents hadn't bothered to tell him that they were coming to our house today too."

Mandie had stood listening to the conversation, and now she looked at the new girl, who was staring at her.

"I'm sorry," Joe said. "Mandie and Irene, this is Lucinda McGoochin. That's Lucinda's brother, Michael, over there playing with the dog."

"Hello," Mandie said, looking at Lucinda.

Mandie felt dowdy in comparison with the finely dressed girl. Lucinda was wearing a silk dress that showed beneath her coat, and she had shiny patent leather shoes on her dainty feet.

Irene kept watching the road. Lucinda was quiet.

"You might as well sit down with us. We're supposed to wait out here until everyone arrives," Joe told Mandie. "You too, Irene."

Mandie sat down in the swing next to Lucinda. The girl was either shy or didn't want to be friendly, Mandie decided.

Leaning forward to look at Joe, Mandie said, "The cat didn't come back."

Lucinda looked at Mandie. "You have a cat? I love cats. We used to have three, and now we don't have any."

"We don't have one either," Mandie replied. "I wish we did. I've always wanted a cat."

"We have six dogs," Lucinda said. "Four of them are my father's hunting dogs and the other two are just little mixed-breed puppies. But still, they are adorable."

Another wagon came down the Woodards' driveway. Mandie instantly knew who it was because Irene broke out in a big grin.

"Hello, Irene," Tommy said.

"Hello, Tommy," Irene replied, her cheeks flushing.

The other four people in the wagon were probably Tommy's parents and grandparents. Mandie didn't know them.

Dr. Woodard had heard the wagon and rushed out to greet them. "Alight! Come in the house," he said as they stepped down from the vehicle. "Glad y'all could come. Everyone's in the house but the young ones here. And they will probably come inside when that food gets on the table." He looked at the young people and smiled.

"I'm sure about that," Joe said.

Mandie turned to look for Irene. She and Tommy were sitting on a rock wall down the driveway, already deep in conversation. Mandie wondered what they could be discussing. They seemed to talk all the time when they got together.

Another buggy was coming down the long driveway, and as it got nearer Mandie became excited. It was Miss Abigail! Joe jumped up and took the reins as she pulled the vehicle to a stop at the stepping block.

"I'm glad you could come, Miss Abigail," Joe told her as he helped her down. "I'll take care of your buggy."

Dr. Woodard instantly appeared in the driveway and escorted the lady inside. Mandie gazed at her with admiration. Miss Abigail not only owned a grand house filled with priceless things, she was a beautiful lady. Everyone wondered why she had never married. Mandie had overheard married women talking about Miss Abigail and wondering why she had never had a husband.

"I believe she is the last guest to arrive," Joe remarked as he handed the reins of Miss Abigail's buggy over to Mr. Miller.

"Then I will put it away and go inside and see what I can do to help out in there," Mr. Miller replied as he jumped into the buggy and drove it on down the driveway.

"I believe we should all go inside now too," Joe told his friends. "Won't be long until all that delicious food is served." He smiled at Mandie and Lucinda. Then he called to Irene and Tommy, "Let's go in the house. It's food time."

All the young people followed Joe inside. A man and woman who Mandie supposed were Lucinda's parents were talking to Tommy Lester's family. Mandie paused just inside the parlor doorway as Joe and Lucinda walked ahead and Irene and Tommy passed her.

"I just don't know what's going on these days," Mrs. McGoochin was saying with a deep frown. "People have become so barbaric. There were at least twenty cats in the community where we live. We had three ourselves and they all disappeared overnight. Not a single cat left in the neighborhood, and we do need cats to get rid of rats and such. What a shame."

Mandie immediately felt her heart beat faster. Someone had stolen all those cats. Maybe the cat she had found was one of the missing cats! But it was a long way to Macon County, where the McGoochins lived. Who would steal a cat and bring it all the way over into Swain County? She took a deep breath. The cat she found could not possibly be from a place that far off, she decided.

Joe turned back and saw Mandie standing there. "Come on. Let's get over next to the dining room door out of the way. Then we'll be in line for food." He grinned.

Mandie grinned back at him. "Maybe you've forgotten, Joe Woodard, but courtesy demands the adults go first."

"I know," he agreed. "But we can at least be ready when our turn comes. Come on."

Mandie followed him over to where Lucinda,

Michael, Irene, and Tommy were standing. But even the aroma of Mrs. Woodard's cooking couldn't stop one question from floating through Mandie's mind: What could have happened to so many cats?

5

The New Arrival

IT WAS LATE that night when the Shaws returned home from visiting the Woodards, but Mandie was determined to go to the barn and check on the cat. Maybe it had come back, she told herself, wishing that was the case.

Mr. Shaw pulled the wagon to a stop at the back door, and Mrs. Shaw and Irene stepped down into the yard. Mandie crawled over the seat to sit next to her father.

"Come on, Amanda," her mother called.

"I want to go with Daddy to take the wagon to the barn," Mandie told her, glancing up at her father in the dim moonlight.

Mrs. Shaw nodded, following Irene to the back door. Mr. Shaw smiled down at his daughter as he shook the reins and headed the wagon toward the barn.

"So you want to check on that cat, is that it?" he asked.

"I thought maybe it might have come back," Mandie replied.

He stopped the wagon in the middle of the barn and jumped down with the lantern. "Well, I hope for your sake it has, Amanda," he said as he began unharnessing the horse.

Mandie darted around the barn, looking into the stalls and into the chicken coop, but she couldn't find the cat anywhere. With a disappointed sigh, she called, "Kitty, kitty, are you here?"

Mr. Shaw rubbed down Dangit and put him in his stall. When he was finished he took the lantern down from the nail where he had hung it and walked over to Mandie, who was standing in the middle of the barn's storage section.

"I'm sorry, dear, but it seems that cat just hasn't come back," he told her, patting her blond head.

Mandie looked up at him as the lantern cast shadows into corners. "Maybe it will be back tomorrow," she said. "Maybe . . ." She stopped and listened. "I hear something!" she cried excitedly.

"So do I. Sounds like a cat to me," Mr. Shaw said with a grin.

"Kitty, kitty, where are you?" Mandie called, searching the barn.

Suddenly the sound was louder. It seemed to come from right over her head. She ran for the ladder. "The cat's in the loft!" she exclaimed.

"Be careful now," Mr. Shaw warned as he watched her climb.

The cat sat at the top of the ladder, growling softly.

"What is it, kitty? Are you sick?" Mandie whispered, coming alongside it.

The cat growled even more loudly and backed away from Mandie as she stepped off the ladder into the hay. Mandie followed, then suddenly stopped. "Daddy! Daddy!" she screamed. "It's got a little kitten up here!"

The cat had moved away from Mandie and picked up the kitten in its mouth.

Mr. Shaw climbed up the ladder with the lantern. "The mother is afraid you will take her baby away from her, Amanda," he explained. "The best way to handle this is to go get some food and put it up here in the loft where she can keep her kitten safe from other animals."

"Oh, Daddy, isn't it wonderful? Now I have two cats, or rather a cat and a kitten. I wish she would let me hold it," Mandie said wistfully. The cat had sat down at the rear of the loft, still holding her tiny, light-colored kitten and never taking her eyes off Mandie and Mr. Shaw.

"Not now. Come on. The mother is probably hungry," Mr. Shaw told Mandie as he turned to go back down the ladder.

Back in the kitchen Mandie excitedly told her mother and Irene about the kitten as her father got scraps of food out of the warmer.

"What color is the kitten?" Irene asked. But she didn't seem truly interested.

"It was dark up there with just that one lantern, but it looked yellowish," Mandie said with a big smile. She filled a small bucket with water to take to the cat.

"Just you be sure that cat doesn't get in this

house with that kitten," her mother reminded her.

"Yes, ma'am," Mandie replied. "I'll watch out for them."

"Come on, Amanda," Mr. Shaw said, picking up the bowl of food he had prepared. "Starting tomorrow you should take a bowl of milk out there every day for the mother cat so she will be able to feed her kitten."

"Yes, sir, I will," Mandie promised, following her father out the back door, a pail of water in her hands. She stopped and turned back to look at her mother. "Thank you, Mama, for letting me keep the cat."

Her mother gave her a smile. "Only on conditions that I have mentioned before will you be allowed to keep that cat. Now, get a move on. It's past bedtime," she said.

"And don't be too long," Irene said to Mandie. "I'm going to bed and I don't want you to come in late and wake me up."

"All right, all right, I'll hurry," Mandie promised.

When they got back to the barn, Mr. Shaw

helped Mandie carry the water and the food up the ladder. The mother cat watched every move they made from her spot in the back corner with her kitten.

"Come on, kitty," Mandie tried to coax her. "We have food over here."

"Let's just let her alone tonight, Amanda," her father said. "She knows we have food, and if we put it over here in the corner I'm sure she will eat it as soon as we leave." He pushed hay out of a corner to clear a spot for the bowl and bucket.

After leaving the food and water, Mr. Shaw and Mandie started down the ladder. When they reached the bottom, Mandie stood on tiptoe, trying to see back up into the loft.

"It's late, Amanda. We should go back and get some sleep," her father told her. "Tomorrow is Saturday. You'll have plenty of time to come back to check on them." Carrying the lantern, he led the way out of the barn.

"I'm so excited about the kitten I probably won't sleep much tonight," Mandie told him as she grasped his free hand.

"After all that socializing at the Woodards' I

think I will be glad to get some peaceful sleep," her father told her. They went through the back door of the house.

"Good night, Daddy," Mandie said as she started up the ladder to the room she shared with her sister.

"Good night, dear. Sweet dreams," her father said as he went on to his room.

Mandie wanted to stay awake and think about the wonderful little kitten. How would it feel if she could just touch it? Would it make friends with her? Would the mother allow Mandie to pick it up?

She was dreaming about holding the tiny kitten when the rooster in the backyard woke her early the next morning.

While Irene slept, Mandie got dressed and hurried down the ladder. The smell of coffee told her that her father was already up. And when she entered the kitchen she found her mother there also.

"Good morning, Mama. Good morning, Daddy."

Mr. Shaw smiled. "I know you are real anxious about that kitten, so go ahead and check on it, but hurry back."

"Yes, we have lots to do today with all those people coming to visit tonight," Mrs. Shaw said as she took a pot down from a hook.

"Are we having company tonight?" Mandie asked.

"The Woodards and the McGoochins," her mother said.

"The McGoochins?" Mandie repeated.

"Yes, that's what I just said," Mrs. Shaw replied.

Mandie frowned as she went outside. *The McGoochins are coming to eat at our house tonight.* She had not really made friends with Lucinda or her brother the night before. They didn't seem to have anything in common with Mandie and Mandie had not had much to say to them. She had noticed that even Joe had little to say to them, although the families had known each other for years. The McGoochins were not friendly like Mandie and her family.

"Oh, well, maybe they won't stay long," Mandie said to herself as she hurried on toward the barn.

As she came to the doorway Mandie slowed down, not wanting to scare the cat. She walked slowly to the ladder and climbed up to the loft. She could hear the mother cat purring to her baby—and could hear the baby making weak meows.

"Good morning, kitty," Mandie said in a low voice as she stopped on the top rung of the ladder. The mother cat was lying near the bowl, which was now empty, and the kitten was curled up next to her. When the cat started to move away Mandie whispered, "Don't move, Mama kitty. I just wanted to see if you were still here. I have to go back and eat breakfast, but just as soon as I finish I promise I'll bring some food for you. You stay right there and don't run away, now."

Mandie softly descended the ladder and then raced back to the house.

"Daddy, the cat ate the food we took out there last night," she said, rushing into the kitchen.

"I figured it would," he said.

"Speaking of food, go wake your sister. We're about ready to eat," her mother told her as she put dishes on the table.

But Irene didn't want to get up. She lay there, refusing to budge, until her mother came to yell up the ladder. "Irene, get down here immediately! Breakfast is waiting, and I need lots of help today for all that company coming tonight."

"The McGoochins and the Woodards are coming to supper," Mandie told her sister.

Irene sat up, yawned, and stretched. "Anybody else?"

Mandie shrugged. "That's all, I suppose. You're wondering if Tommy and his family are invited, aren't you? I don't think so."

"Then don't count on me being around too much tonight. I'm sure Tommy will come by, and when he does I'll just—disappear, you know," Irene said, jumping up and putting on her clothes.

"Mama might not like that, Irene," Mandie told her.

"Mama probably won't even notice if I'm not around," Irene replied, buttoning up her dress. "Are that cat and its kitten still out there in the barn?"

Mandie grinned. "They sure are. I've already been out there this morning."

Irene grinned back. "Maybe I'll stay out there and guard them for you tonight so all those people can't disturb them."

"Oh, would you, Irene? The mother is so jittery about her kitten. A lot of people would frighten her, and she might run away again," Mandie told her.

"Don't tell any of those people about the cat and its kitten. I'll stay out there watching just in case someone comes to the barn," Irene promised as she slipped on her shoes.

"Hurry up, girls!" Mrs. Shaw called from the bottom of the ladder.

Mandie rushed back down to the kitchen, and Irene followed. As everyone sat down to eat, Mandie thought about Irene's offer. Why was Irene willing to stay out at the barn for hours to protect the cat and her kitten from their visitors? Her sister did not even like the cat. Irene was probably meeting Tommy out there.

"Amanda, eat up. We've got lots of work to do," Mrs. Shaw told her.

Mandie quickly picked up her fork and dug into the grits on her plate. "Oh, well," she mumbled to herself as she glanced at her sister across the table. Irene was devouring everything in front of her. If Irene was willing to help, Mandie would certainly accept it.

As soon as breakfast was over, Mrs. Shaw sent Mandie and Irene to the smokehouse to straighten things up there. Mandie was allowed to feed the cat first.

Mandie looked around inside the smokehouse and saw things out of place. A huge slab of bacon was hanging in the middle of the hamhocks. Ears of multicolored Indian corn, hung up to dry out, and used to make strings of kernels at Christmas to put on the tree were scattered around the room. People got in a hurry when they went to fetch something from the smokehouse or to add to its stock. Things were in a mixed-up mess.

"I'll do this side if you want to do that side over there," Mandie told her sister. Irene was walking between the racks that stood in the middle of the floor.

Irene looked at her for a moment. "You go ahead and start. I've got to run and get a drink of water."

Before Mandie could answer, Irene had

darted out the door and disappeared. So Mandie began to put the place in some kind of order by herself. She worked for a long time before realizing that Irene was not coming back. "I hope Irene doesn't go to the barn and disturb the cat and her kitten," she said as she gave the floor a final sweep. When she finally finished, she hurried out to the barn.

Running across the back yard, Mandie saw her father in the far-distant field, working on the fence again. As he looked her way, they exchanged waves. But she didn't see Irene anywhere. And she was not in the barn. The cat was curled up asleep, her paw holding her baby, when Mandie softly climbed the ladder to check on them. The mother opened one eye to look in her direction, but she didn't move and Mandie didn't disturb them.

"Irene must be in the house. Mama probably gave her another job to do," Mandie said to herself as she slipped back down the ladder and headed for the back door of the house.

When she entered the kitchen she found her mother in the middle of baking cakes and pies. The sweet smell made Mandie hungry.

Her mother glanced at her as she whipped batter. "Y'all finished with the smokehouse? Now I'd like you and your sister to go out and sweep the yard, front and back. And don't leave a single chestnut on the ground. Remember, the old people could trip over them and fall."

"But, Mama . . ." Mandie was about to say that she didn't know where her sister was but realized Irene would be in trouble if she told on her.

"No buts about it," her mother said, pouring the batter into cake pans. "Now, go on and get it over with."

"Yes, ma'am," Mandie said as she picked up a broom from the corner and went back outside.

Mandie viciously swept the yard as she fussed to herself. "Going off and leaving me to do all the work," she mumbled. "Just wait. I'll get even with her next time. I'll run off before she has a chance to. That's what I'll do." She gave a hard push with the broom, and several chestnuts went flying into the field nearby.

Although Mandie had to sweep the whole yard by herself, she finished quickly. Leaving the broom on the front porch, she rushed off down to the barn to check one more time on the cat and her kitten.

This time the mother was awake and busily washing her kitten as she purred to it. After a quick glance at Mandie, the cat continued her job while Mandie watched in fascination.

Suddenly Mandie heard a giggle in the barn below her. She turned to look down and saw Irene run out of the barn with Tommy Lester chasing after her. *So that's where she's been!* Mandie thought. *While I'm working she's out having a good time. I'll get even with her!*

6

Emergency

LATER THAT AFTERNOON Joe Woodard came to Mandie's house. She had just started across the yard toward the barn when she saw him hurrying down the pathway from the road.

"Oh, Joe, I have something to show you!" Mandie exclaimed. She stood there waiting. "Come on."

"Wait, Mandie," Joe told her. "I have a message from my mother to your mother. My father had an emergency sick call to make and we probably won't get here tonight until about six o'clock."

Mandie nodded. "I'll tell my mother. What time had you planned to come over?" she asked as they walked toward the back door.

"My mother said we were expected by five o'clock at the latest," Joe said.

When Mandie opened the back door, the aroma from Mrs. Shaw's baking wafted out to greet them. Joe patted his stomach. "Oh, boy, I hope we're not too late getting here tonight, with all that baking your mother is doing. I can't wait to eat half of everything." He grinned down at Mandie.

Mandie smiled up at him as they stepped inside the kitchen.

"Well, I sure hope everyone has not come early. It's only three o'clock and I'm not finished with the food yet," Mrs. Shaw told him, her eyes teasing. She swiped the worktable with the dishrag in her hand.

"Oh, no, ma'am, Mrs. Shaw. I'm the only one here. My father had to go out on an emergency call and my mother sent me to tell you we won't be here until about six o'clock," Joe explained.

"That's fine, Joe. You just go back and tell your mother that won't be a problem at all. We'll see y'all then, and if y'all are a little later than six, don't worry about it. We understand," Mrs. Shaw told him. She opened the oven door to check on her baking.

"Thank you, Mrs. Shaw. I can't wait to sample everything I smell baking," Joe said eagerly.

Mrs. Shaw straightened up and smiled at him. "We're going to have plenty, Joe. Plan on eating all you want."

"Come on, Joe," Mandie urged, tugging on Joe's sleeve. "I want to show you something." She led the way outside.

"All right, but I do have to hurry back home," Joe replied. He trailed after Mandie as she practically ran to the barn.

"Stop right here, and please be quiet," Mandie told him, standing at the doorway.

"That cat must have come back," Joe guessed.

"Yes, and she's in the loft, so we have to be very quiet or she might run away again," Mandie cautioned. She softly entered the barn and went to the ladder. Joe followed.

Mandie began quietly climbing the ladder and motioned for Joe to follow her. When she reached the top she saw the cat curled up with her kitten in the corner. Mandie moved a little to the side. "Look back there!"

Joe peered over her shoulder into the loft. "A

kitten! That's great! The mother cat will probably stay here with y'all now."

"I hope so," Mandie replied. She watched the tiny golden kitten move closer to its mother. The mother began purring to it as she washed its head.

Joe started back down the ladder. "I'm so glad about the kitten," he told Mandie as she followed him down into the barn. "But remember what Mrs. McGoochin said about all those cats that were missing in her community? This cat could be one of them."

Mandie stomped her foot. "Oh, Joe, I hope nobody claims her. How could this cat have come all the way from over the mountain in Macon County anyhow?"

Joe walked outside the barn, and Mandie followed. "Well now, you know that cat had to come from somewhere. Why don't you at least let Mrs. McGoochin have a look? She might recognize it."

"We-e-l-l-l . . ." Mandie drew the word out as she frowned. "I suppose I should, but I hate to think someone might claim her."

"Mandie, look at it this way. If that was your

cat and it had disappeared, you would want whoever found it to let you know, wouldn't you?" Joe argued.

Mandie sighed. "All right, Joe, I suppose you're right—but I sure hope Mrs. McGoochin doesn't recognize her," she said. She had fallen in love with the cat—and especially the kitten. How could she give them up now?

"Tonight, when everyone is busy in the house, you could get a private word with Mrs. McGoochin. Ask her to come out here and look at it," Joe suggested. "And if she doesn't know anything about the cat, then you'll feel more free about keeping it."

"But if she does know who the cat belongs to, I'll have to give her up," Mandie said wistfully. She took a deep breath. "I'll do the right thing, Joe."

Joe gave her a big grin and started toward the pathway to the road. "I knew Mandie Shaw was an honest person. See you tonight." He waved at her.

Mandie waved back. Sometimes it was terrible having to be honest, but she had to do this. She started toward the back door.

In her room upstairs Mandie quickly put on a fresh navy dress with white frills around the neck and sleeves. She tied back her long blond hair with a matching piece of navy, cut from the material when the dress had been made the month before. The dress was really her Sunday-go-to-meeting dress, but her mother had wanted her to wear it that night, since Lucinda McGoochin was bound to be dressed in her best.

Irene finally made an appearance. "Why are you all dressed up?" she asked as Mandie buttoned her dress.

"Mama said we should try to look our best so the McGoochins won't think we are poor," Mandie explained. "Irene, we are not really poor, are we?" She frowned.

Irene grabbed one of her best dresses from a hanger. "I don't think so. We always have plenty to eat, and heat in the winter and all that. No, I don't think we're poor." She took off the dress she had on, pulled the clean dress over her head, and straightened out the folds of the skirt.

"I'm not sure what being poor really is, but I do believe the McGoochins must be wealthy, judging from the way they dress," Mandie said. Then she remembered Irene's absence all day and her own promise to Joe to talk to Mrs. McGoochin. "While you have been out running around with Tommy Lester all day, I had to do all the work," she informed her sister. "And as far as you watching the cat tonight, just forget about that. Joe came by here this afternoon and I agreed to ask Mrs. McGoochin to look at the cat to see if it belongs to her or someone she knows." She stopped to catch her breath after her hurried speech—she had spoken quickly to keep Irene from interrupting.

Irene made a face. "I haven't been out with Tommy all afternoon. And he won't be here tonight, so just forget about the offer I made to watch the cat. Silly old cat, anyway. Maybe it'll go back where it came from." She put on her best shoes and buttoned them up.

"Well, that settles that, then," Mandie curtly told her. She hurried to the ladder and went downstairs without giving Irene a chance to say anything more. Because of Irene's undisciplined ways, Mandie always thought of her as being broken down and in need of repair. However, she wasn't sure what repairs should be made. So she usually just walked off and left Irene to herself when Irene got cranky.

At six o'clock on the dot the Woodards and the McGoochins arrived at the Shaws' home. Mandie watched through the parlor window as they pulled up, then ran into the kitchen, where her mother was putting the finishing touches on the table. "They're here," Mandie cried before hurrying out the back door.

Mr. Shaw was outside helping the ladies step down from the wagon. "Go right on in. I believe Etta's in the kitchen," he told Mrs. Woodard and Mrs. McGoochin as they walked toward the house.

Dr. Woodard threw the reins to Joe. "You take care of it, son."

"Yes, sir," Joe replied. As he started toward the barn with the wagon, Lucinda and Michael yelled for him to let them out.

"I don't want to ride to the barn, Joe. Leave me here," Lucinda said, lifting her long, full skirts and jumping down to the ground.

"Neither do I," Michael said, following his sister.

"Be right back," Joe called as he drove the wagon on down the lane.

Mandie breathed a sigh of relief. If the McGoochins had gone to the barn, they might have discovered the cat! "I'll wait for you," she called to Joe. Lucinda and Michael had already hurried to the back door. The two didn't seem very friendly. Maybe they were upset about something.

When Joe came back up the lane he told Mandie, "Everyone is all excited, or I should say worried. My dad's emergency patient this afternoon was a boy over in the mountain who is very ill with the measles, and you know that stuff is contagious. So Mr. and Mrs. McGoochin are anxious to get back home for fear Lucinda and Michael might catch the disease from my dad."

"Oh, I am sorry," Mandie said. "I could tell something was wrong."

"I suppose we don't worry too much at our house because my dad is always treating people with diseases," Joe said.

Mandie wasn't worried either. "Let's go inside. Maybe I can get a chance to speak to Mrs. McGoochin about the cat," Mandie told him.

Inside the house Mandie found Irene entertaining the two young McGoochins with some wild story she was making up. Lucinda and Michael sat near Irene in the parlor and were so absorbed in Irene's tale that they didn't even look at Mandie and Joe when they came into the room.

"Let's leave them here," Mandie whispered to Joe.

Joe followed Mandie into the kitchen, where the women were discussing the measles while Mrs. Shaw was taking the food from the stove to put on the table.

"When I was young there was an epidemic. Several of my friends died from measles," Mrs. McGoochin was saying as she helped carry the dishes.

"But things are better now," Mrs. Woodard said. "Doctors know more now and can control it better."

"Maybe that's just an isolated case and it won't spread any further," Mrs. Shaw told them. She looked across the room and saw

Mandie and Joe standing inside the doorway. "Amanda, you and Joe go let out the table in the parlor. You younguns can eat in there."

"Yes, ma'am," Mandie said. She'd have to speak to Mrs. McGoochin later.

"We'll get it done," Joe told her.

Irene helped them clear the books off the drop-leaf table in the parlor and put up the leaves.

Several minutes later, Mrs. Shaw stuck her head in the door. "Come ahead and get your food."

The five young people quickly filled their plates in the kitchen and took them back to the table in the parlor. Mandie kept trying to catch Mrs. McGoochin when she wasn't busy talking, but she seemed to be talking to somebody every minute.

Irene was still telling tales to Lucinda and Michael while they were eating, so Mandie had a chance to whisper to Joe. "I don't believe I'll ever get to ask her tonight," she said, taking a spoonful of beans.

"It can wait," Joe said under his breath. "They're planning to come back in two weeks—

that is, if we don't have a measles outbreak. Mrs. McGoochin is helping my mother make some fancy table scarves for somebody who is getting married, and she will have her part all done by then."

Mandie smiled at him. "Then I'll get to keep the cat at least two more weeks for sure."

"Just don't get attached too much to it," Joe warned her. "It must belong to somebody somewhere, and the owner may show up any day."

"I know," Mandie agreed.

As soon as the meal was over, the McGoochins and the Woodards left. After seeing them off, Mr. Shaw told Mandie, "Get some scraps for the cat and I'll go with you to feed it while I have the lantern handy."

Mandie found lots of scraps! Evidently the McGoochins had not enjoyed their food very much.

As Mandie walked with her father toward the barn, she told him that she had agreed with Joe to show Mrs. McGoochin the cat to see whether she recognized her or not. "But everyone was in such a hurry, I didn't get a chance to ask her," Mandie fretted.

"You probably heard Mrs. McGoochin tell your mother they would be back in two weeks, so you can take care of that then," Mr. Shaw replied. "I hope for your sake that no one claims the cat, but you know it is tame and therefore must belong to someone."

"Yes, sir," Mandie said, looking up at her father in the light from the lantern he was carrying. "Maybe whoever the cat belongs to will give her to me. Maybe they don't want her anymore," she added.

"That's a possibility, but don't count on it," he said as they entered the barn.

The cat was curled up in the corner and the kitten was asleep next to her. As she placed the food in the bowl, Mandie hoped with all her heart that she could keep them forever.

7

Damaged Yarn

MANDIE GOT UP early Monday to check on the cat and her kitten before breakfast. When she opened the back door to go outside, the cat was sitting on the doorstep, the tiny kitten dangling from her mouth.

"Oh, my goodness, I'm glad Mama didn't find you out here," Mandie whispered. She bent to pat the cat's head, surprised that the cat allowed her to touch her. "Come on. We've got to go back to the barn," she said, coaxing the cat to follow her.

But the cat just sat and watched. Finally Mandie tried to pick her up. But the cat had other ideas. She immediately jumped up and ran down the lane to the barn, still holding the kitten by its neck. Mandie followed.

She found her father milking the cow in the

barn. First the cat circled around Mr. Shaw. Then she went over to a corner and, laying down the kitten, sat and watched him.

"Daddy, the cat came to the house with her kitten," Mandie said.

"She's probably hungry. Run and get her bowl out of the loft and I'll fill it up with milk," Mr. Shaw replied.

Mandie quickly got the bowl. Her father filled it with milk straight from the cow and put it down near the cat.

"Move back a little," her father told her. "The cat still doesn't exactly trust us."

Mandie stepped nearer to her father and watched the cat hungrily lap the milk. "Daddy, the cat was on the back doorstep. I'm so glad Mama didn't find her out there," she said. "Could you please watch out for the cat in case she goes back up to the house while I'm at school?"

"Sure I will," he said, smiling. "I don't think your mother will say anything as long as the cat doesn't get inside the house."

"Thank you, Daddy," Mandie said. "I'll hurry home to look after her."

Mandie worried all through school that day. *If the cat gets into the house, Mama will make me get rid of her,* she thought nervously. As soon as Mr. Tallant dismissed them, she hurried home from school. Her mother was standing on the front porch.

"That cat got in this house, and I told you to keep it out." Mrs. Shaw started fussing as soon as Mandie got to the front steps. "Not only that, it brought that kitten in the house!"

Mandie held her breath. She'd never seen her mother so upset. "I'm sorry, Mama," she said meekly.

"Don't just stand there. Get in this house and find that kitten," her mother told her as she opened the front door and went into the parlor.

Mandie followed, hastily throwing her books on a chair. "The kitten? Is the cat in here too?" she asked, looking around the room.

"No, I was able to shoo the cat outside, but I couldn't find that kitten. It's in here somewhere. Now, you find it immediately," Mrs. Shaw said. She went over to her yarn basket sitting by a chair and pulled out some yarn. Instead of being in a ball, though, the yarn was torn apart. "I've got to go to the country store and see if I can match up some of this yarn," her mother said, frowning. "Something has been chewing on it." She continued looking through the basket.

Mandie gasped. "Did the cat do that?"

"No, I found this before the cat got in the house, and I know the cat was out in the yard all morning because I was watching it to be sure it didn't get inside. But I had my hands full when I took the scraps to the hogs and I had to leave the door open just a little. So I suppose that cat crept inside then. Unless you let it in and I didn't know it."

"Mama, I have not let the cat in at any time. I'm sorry," Mandie said. "And I'm sorry about your yarn, but I can't imagine what happened to that, unless it was a rat—"

"Rat?" Mrs. Shaw interrupted. "Young lady, there are no rats in here. I keep a clean house." She looked out the window. "Your father is out there with the wagon to take me to the store. Now, you get busy and find that kitten before I get back, you hear me?" She pulled out a few strands of yarn to take with her.

"Yes, ma'am," Mandie replied.

Her mother went outside, and Mandie watched from the window to be sure she left. As soon as the wagon was out of sight Mandie ran to the barn.

"The only way I know how to find that little kitten is to get the mother cat to hunt it. I'm sure she's worried about her kitten being missing," Mandie said to herself as she reached the barn doors.

A loud meow greeted Mandie as she stepped inside. The cat came running to meet her. Looking up at Mandie, she meowed loudly. Mandie stooped down to pat her head. "I know you are looking for your kitten," she told the cat. Leaning forward, she tried to pick her up. The cat backed off a little but continued looking up at Mandie and meowing.

"Well, come on then," Mandie told the cat. She started to the door of the barn, and the cat followed her. "That's right. You just follow me—but we've got to hurry. Come on." She began walking briskly back toward the house.

When she got to the back door, she opened it

and the cat quickly pushed past her into the kitchen. Mandie watched as the cat ran around meowing and sniffing everything in the room. Then the cat ran into the parlor and went straight to Mrs. Shaw's yarn basket.

"Please don't mess up Mama's yarn or she will be awfully mad," Mandie told the cat.

"Meow!"

To Mandie's surprise, a rat ran out from under the chair by the yarn basket! The cat tried to pounce on it, but at that very moment the kitten meowed with all its might from somewhere on the other side of the room. The cat immediately let the rat get away to go to her baby.

"Now we have a rat in here and I won't be able to find it!" *And if I did I wouldn't know what to do about it, and Mama is never going to believe me if I tell her,* Mandie thought, glancing around the floor.

The mother cat suddenly leapt into the woodbox by the fireplace and came back out with her kitten in her mouth. She looked at Mandie and ran into the kitchen and to the back door.

"That's good," Mandie told the cat, hurrying

after her to open the door. "You know your kitten doesn't belong in here. So you just take it back to the barn now, you hear?" She bent to look at the cat as she talked.

The minute the door was open the cat streaked through, still carrying her kitten. Mandie breathed a sigh of relief as she leaned against the closed door. "At least the cat is out of the house. But what am I going to do about that rat?" She shivered as she thought about the horrible rat.

At that moment Irene came in through the front door. "Well, what are *you* doing? Propping up the door?" Irene asked, looking at Mandie.

Mandie straightened up. "I might as well tell you. The cat got in the house with her kitten while we were at school today. Mama got the cat out and couldn't find the kitten. I just now found it, and the cat has taken it back to the barn."

"She told you not to let that cat in the house," Irene reminded her. "Is Mama going to make you get rid of it?"

Mandie was upset over what her mother

might do, but she didn't want Irene to know. She took a deep breath. "I suppose I'll find out when she gets back from the store."

"She's gone to the store?" Irene asked, opening the warmer and selecting a biscuit. Then, going over to the pie safe, she took out a jar of molasses and, after splitting the biscuit in half, poured a dab of the molasses on it and put it back together.

Mandie wondered why her sister was so hungry after all the food she had taken to school for noontime recess. She always took double what Mandie did and only gave Tommy half of it.

"Daddy took her in the wagon. She needed to buy some yarn," Mandie replied after a pause. She knew she couldn't trust her sister not to use anything Mandie did or said to her own advantage with their mother.

"Yarn? My goodness, her basket is running over with yarn. What does she want with more?" Irene asked as she ate the biscuit.

Mandie sighed. "Something got in her yarn and chewed it. And it wasn't the cat, because Mama found the yarn before the cat got in the house."

Irene made a face. "A rat?"

"That's what I said, but Mama says there are no rats in our house," Mandie told her.

"Well, I hope not," Irene said, swallowing the last bite of the biscuit.

Mandie had a sudden idea. "Why don't you get Tommy Lester to come in and look around while Mama is gone, just to be sure?" she asked her sister.

Irene frowned and then smiled. "All right. He's waiting for me down at the spring. I'll be right back." Shaking the crumbs from her dress, she ran out the back door.

While Mandie waited for her to return, she decided that maybe involving Tommy was a dumb idea. Suppose her mother came back while Tommy Lester was in the house? Mrs. Shaw did not allow Mandie's or Irene's friends in the house when she was not there. Mandie's sister would get in trouble if her mother found out.

But it was too late. Irene was back in a few minutes. Tommy Lester, tall, gangly, and dark, followed her through the back door and looked around.

"You say there might be a rat in the house?" he asked Mandie.

Mandie quickly went to the yarn basket and showed him the damaged yarn.

He smiled. "Sure looks like a rat has been at work on that. Now, what we need to do is scatter out in different rooms. I'll begin beating around on everything, and you girls keep an eye out for a rat."

Mandie was embarrassed to tell him she had already seen a rat, especially when her mother had emphatically denied having such a thing in her house. She bit her lip. "What do we do if we see a rat?"

"I have an idea, Mandie," Irene said. "Why don't you go get that cat, and then if we do find a rat it will catch it for us?"

"Mama has forbidden me to let the cat in the house," Mandie reminded her. "We'll just have to beat it with a broom or something if we do find a rat."

"Grab something to swat it with," Tommy said. He began banging on walls, shaking chairs and tables, and stomping on the floor as he worked his way through the house. The girls grabbed the dishrags and watched.

As Tommy banged, Mandie happened to glance out a window. Her father and mother were pulling up to the back door in their wagon! She ran to hush Tommy. "Quick! You'd better get out the front door. Mama and Daddy are at the back." She hurried to straighten the furniture.

Irene grabbed Tommy's hand. "Come on. We'll go outside," she told him. The two raced out the front door and closed it behind them as Mrs. Shaw came in the back door, carrying an armful of yarn.

"At least I was able to match most of the yarn," Mrs. Shaw said, seeing Mandie standing there. She laid her purchases on the kitchen table. "I'll have to clean out the basket."

"I'm glad you could find the right yarn, Mama," Mandie said.

"And did you find that kitten?" her mother asked as she took off her coat.

"Yes, ma'am," Mandie replied. "The cat and the kitten are both back out in the barn."

Mrs. Shaw frowned as she looked at Mandie. "What was all that noise I heard when we drove up? It sounded like somebody was banging on the walls."

Mandie took a deep breath. "Mama—"

Just then the door opened and her father came into the kitchen. "Sure seems like it's getting colder out there. I wouldn't be surprised if we got some snow." He went to the cookstove, which was kept going all winter, and warmed his hands.

Mrs. Shaw, apparently forgetting about her question, picked up the percolator and shook it. "I believe there's at least two cups in here," she said. "Amanda, get cups for your father and me and one for you if you want coffee." She set the pot back on the stove and took the yarn off the table, depositing it in a nearby chair.

Mandie went to the cupboard and took down the dishes. "I don't believe I want any, Mama," she said. "I need to do my homework right now." She started toward the door to the parlor.

"That's a good girl," Mrs. Shaw said, picking

up the pot and filling the cups. She and Mr. Shaw sat down at the table.

"You say Mr. Henry said that yarn looked like rats had got in it?" Mr. Shaw asked his wife. Mandie stopped to listen.

"Yes, and I told him he didn't know what he was talking about. There are no rats in my house," Mrs. Shaw said, taking a sip of coffee.

"Now, I don't know of any way you can be sure of that. Rats can find their way into almost anything," Mr. Shaw replied.

"I'm not going to argue about it. There are no rats in my house," Mandie's mother insisted. "Now, have you heard any more from Dr. Woodard about that measles patient he has?"

"No, not a word," Mr. Shaw said, shaking his head.

As Mandie sat down in the parlor to do her homework, she had a sudden idea. She would tell her father that she definitely had seen a rat in the house. Maybe he could take her mother off somewhere again and Mandie could bring the cat into the house to hunt it!

In the meantime, Mandie was afraid to put

her feet on the floor while she sat doing her homework, for fear the rat would run across them. She shivered and tried to keep her mind on her books. The very first chance she had to get her father alone, she would talk to him. That would solve the whole problem.

8

Caught!

WHEN MANDIE WENT out to the barn that night to feed the cat, her father went with her to carry the lantern. At last she would get a chance to talk to him alone. She waited until she had fed the cat and they were ready to return to the house.

"Daddy, there's something I need to talk to you about," she said as they walked up the path.

"What is it, dear?"

"It's Mama," Mandie began. "You see, we do have a rat in the house."

"Are you sure?" her father asked.

"Yes, sir," Mandie replied. "I saw it myself! And the cat did too, but when she found her kitten in the woodbox she let the rat go and picked up her kitten instead, so the rat is still in the house."

"Well, we'll just have to do something about that," her father said, frowning. "I'll set some traps after everyone goes to bed."

"But, Daddy, if the trap catches the rat, Mama will probably see it. I have another idea. You take Mama off somewhere for a while tomorrow after I get home from school, and I'll bring the cat in the house. I know that cat will catch it."

Her father nodded. "All right. Your mother and I will run over to the Woodards' for a few minutes tomorrow afternoon. That will give the cat time to find the rat before we come back. That way we won't have to upset your mother about all this."

"I knew you'd understand," Mandie said, reaching out to give her father's hand a squeeze.

Mr. Shaw put one arm around his daughter. "Now, let's get back in the house out of this cold."

Mandie went to bed happy that night. With her father's help everything would come out all right.

★ ★ ★

When she woke the next morning she looked outside and saw everything covered with snow! Large, thick flakes swirled in the air. Mandie loved snow, and she leaned against the glass to look down into the yard. White drifts covered the ground as far as she could see.

"How beautiful!" she exclaimed softly.

Her sister heard her and got out of bed to see what she was talking about.

"Snow!" Irene said, happily dancing around the small room.

"What are you so happy about?" Mandie asked.

"From the looks of things out there, it must have been snowing all night. School may be closed today," Irene told her. She quickly got dressed.

Mandie went over to put on her clothes. "We've had more snow than that out there before and they didn't close the school. After all, Mr. Tallant lives in the school building, so he'll be there regardless."

"Yes, but probably no one will show up for school with that much snow," Irene said, putting on her high-top button shoes.

"We'd better go downstairs and see what Mama and Daddy have to say about it," Mandie told her.

Their parents were already up and cooking breakfast when the girls got down to the kitchen. Before either girl could say a word, their mother told them, "No school today with that snowstorm out there. You girls will have to study at home."

"I'm afraid no one will be out traveling anywhere today," Mr. Shaw said, giving Mandie a wink. "We've already got six inches and there's no sign of its letting up."

Mandie sighed as she understood that her father was telling her the business with the rat would have to wait. He would not be able to take her mother anywhere.

Just as they sat down to breakfast, Joe Woodard came riding up on his horse. He threw the reins over the hitching post and came stamping to the back door. Mr. Shaw went to open it.

"Good morning, sir," Joe greeted him. Flakes of snow blew around him. "I just wanted to let Mandie and Irene know Mr. Tallant has closed the school for today, and it won't reopen until the snow stops and melts off enough for travel."

"Don't stand out there in the snow, Joe. Come on in the house," Mr. Shaw said, pushing the door wide open.

Joe stamped his feet on the stoop and then stepped into the warm room. The heat from the stove immediately melted the flakes that clung to his heavy coat and hat. He looked down at the wet mess in dismay.

"Take off your coat and hat and get over there by the stove," Mr. Shaw told him. Obligingly Joe removed his garments and gave them to Mr. Shaw, who hung them on pegs by the back door.

"Thank you, Mr. Shaw, but I sure hope I'm not messing up Mrs. Shaw's floor with all this snow," Joe said, cautiously walking over to the cookstove.

"Nonsense, boy, get warm and then come over here for a bite to eat. We just sat down. There's plenty for you, too," Mrs. Shaw told him.

After Joe had helped himself to a biscuit, Mr. Shaw asked, "How does it happen that you are out in all this? How did you know Mr. Tallant closed the school? It's not even time for school to open for the day yet."

"My dad was on an early call to the Perringers' near the schoolhouse and he stopped to chat with Mr. Tallant for a few minutes," Joe explained, quickly eating the food on his plate. "I told Dad I would come and let y'all know so Mandie and Irene wouldn't walk all the way to school for nothing."

"I knew school would be out," Irene said smugly.

"Do you have to go back right away?" Mandie asked.

"No, not really. I do have to get home before it gets too bad to travel, though," Joe said.

"When you finish your breakfast we need to put your horse in the barn out of all this," Mr. Shaw told him.

"Yes, sir. That stuff out there is coming down fast," Joe said, taking a sip of coffee.

"We may be in for a big one," Mr. Shaw agreed.

And that's what they did have, a big snow. It

came down for days and days, and no one could go anywhere.

The snow finally quit the next Monday. The sun came out and the weather warmed up enough to begin melting the white cover on the ground. On Wednesday school reopened, and as soon as Mandie got home that afternoon, she was greeted by her mother and father at the back door. "Your father and I are going over to the Woodards' for a few minutes. After being shut in so long, we need to get out of this house," Mrs. Shaw said. "You get your homework done, and tell Irene I said to do hers. We'll be back before suppertime."

"Yes, ma'am," Mandie said. She shared a secret smile with her father.

As soon as they drove out of the yard, Mandie raced to the barn and brought the cat back into the house. The animal had become more friendly and tame with Mandie and even let Mandie pick her up.

"Now, you be a good girl and find that rat that got away from you that day, you hear?"

Mandie told the cat, setting her down in the parlor near the yarn basket. She hoped the cat would find the rat before Irene came home. As usual, her sister had disappeared after school.

The cat looked up at Mandie for a minute and then began roaming the house. Mandie curled up in a chair to do her homework. She was trying to catch up with her reading. Mr. Tallant had overloaded them with work to make up for the snow days. She heard the cat meow now and then, and once she heard her jump. Mandie ran to see what the cat was doing, but she had merely jumped up into the kitchen window and was looking out.

Just as Mandie had settled down once more, there was a loud noise in the kitchen. She ran in. The cat was chasing the rat around the room! Mandie stood back, ready to close the door if the rat came toward her. But the cat knew what she was doing and soon snatched the rat between her teeth. Mandie ran to open the outside door and the cat raced outside, carrying the rat with her. Mandie closed the door and looked out the window. The cat had killed the rat and was playing with it in the yard.

"Good!" Mandie said to herself, wiping her brow. Everything was working out just fine.

Before she knew it her mother and father had returned. She watched out the window as they stopped in the yard. Her father spotted the dead rat right away when he stepped down from the wagon. Mandie saw her mother take a deep breath and wobble on toward the back door.

"Where did that rat come from?" Mrs. Shaw asked Mandie as she stepped inside the kitchen and dropped into a chair.

"It was here in the house and the cat caught it just now," Mandie explained.

"You had that cat in the house again?" Mrs. Shaw asked.

"Yes, ma'am, but just to catch the rat," Mandie explained.

At that moment, as Mr. Shaw opened the back door to come into the kitchen, the mother cat with her kitten in her mouth brushed past his legs and into the room. Mandie looked at her mother and then at her father. She didn't know what to do.

Her mother bent forward in her chair. "Come here, kitty. You deserve a nice reward." The cat stayed back, watching her and holding the kitten.

Mrs. Shaw straightened up and looked at Mandie. "I think we might ought to keep that cat in the house from now on so we won't get any more rats," she said. "Imagine, a rat in this house!"

"Oh, thank you, Mama!" Mandie said excitedly.

"I'll put a box behind the stove where it can sleep at night," Mr. Shaw said, giving his daughter a big smile.

The following Saturday the McGoochins returned to visit with the Woodards. The Shaws invited everyone over for a meal again, only this time it was the noonday meal. The weather was still too bad to be out late at night. The snow had melted, but the wind constantly whistled and bent the trees and bushes. Mandie could hardly stand up in the yard, the wind was so strong.

Mandie remembered her promise to Joe. Today was the day she had to keep it.

The mother cat and her kitten were staying in

the house now, but the mother had to be let out now and then. Mandie found the cat in the barn and carried her back to the house. She knew where the kitten was because she had put it upstairs in the attic in preparation for the McGoochins' visit.

All the women were in the kitchen when Mandie entered through the back door. The McGoochin children were in the parlor with Irene. She went directly in front of Mrs. McGoochin and held out the cat.

"Mrs. McGoochin, here is a cat I found near our school one day, and I thought—"

Mrs. McGoochin reached for the cat. "Oh, Spot, is it really you? Where have you been all this time?" She eagerly hugged the cat and then looked up at Mandie. "Dear, you'll never know how much we appreciate your finding our cat for us. And where did you say you found her?"

Mandie was aware of Joe's big smile as he stood across the room. "I found her in the bushes one day near the schoolhouse. I thought I heard someone in a buggy stop and yell 'Git!' and then I heard the cat meowing. It was hard to catch her, but I finally did," she explained. Her heart fell into her shoes as she realized she would have to give up the cat.

"Someone stole all the cats in our community, and they had to have some way to take them off, so I suppose it was a buggy," Mrs. McGoochin explained, her eyes filling with tears. "But imagine finding Spot all the way over here. Oh, just wait till the children see her!"

Then Mandie remembered the kitten. She would have to give it up also. "Mrs. McGoochin, there's more," she said slowly, her voice sad. "I'll be right back." She hurried up the ladder to her room and returned to the kitchen with the kitten.

"Here, this belongs to you too, I suppose," Mandie said, holding out the squirming little yellow kitten.

Mrs. McGoochin took the kitten. "Oh, yes, in the excitement I had forgotten about that. So she had the kitten? Was there just one?"

"Yes, ma'am, just the one," Mandie replied as tears threatened to flood her blue eyes.

Mrs. McGoochin looked at Mandie for a moment and then held out the kitten. "I don't believe we'll be wanting to take the kitten. Do you think you could find a nice home for it?"

Mandie couldn't believe her eyes and ears. She eagerly took the kitten back from Mrs. McGoochin and held it tight. "Oh, thank you, Mrs. McGoochin! I wanted the kitten so much. Thank you!" In her excitement Mandie quickly bent forward to give Mrs. McGoochin a quick squeeze.

"We'll have to leave the mother with you also, until the kitten gets old enough to wean. Then we'll come back for Spot," Mrs. McGoochin explained.

"That will be fine," Mrs. Shaw said.

Mandie hurried across the room to Joe, holding the kitten up in the air. "It's all mine! It's really and truly mine!"

"Yes," Joe agreed. "Now all you have to do is give it a name."

"A name? Oh, of course. Let's see. It's awfully windy outside. I think I'll just call it Windy because the wind was blowing so hard when it finally became my very own kitten," Mandie said, twirling around and around with the kitten. "We have solved the mystery of the homeless cat at last."

"Now that you have, I have another mystery," Joe said, immediately getting Mandie's attention. "I saw smoke coming out of the old Conley house over at the foot of the mountain this morning. Do you suppose someone has moved into that old dilapidated barn?"

"I don't know, but we can find out," Mandie replied, reaching over to squeeze Joe's hand. "We'll find out."

Is Joe's guess right? Has someone moved into the old Conley house? Find out in *The New Girl*.

Doo-Lollies

In her spare time, Mandie sometimes makes special crafts like these small pom-poms called Doo-Lollies. She uses her Doo-Lollies for decorating things like pillows, scarves, and even her clothes. You can make Doo-Lollies too. Some of the materials you need to make them have sharp edges, so ask an adult to help you.

Materials you will need:
a small cup
a large cup
a sheet of white paper
a pencil
scissors
scraps of colorful cloth
straight pins
a needle
thread

1. Create two patterns by placing the cups on the sheet of paper. For the small circle, use the pencil to trace the bottom of the small cup. For the big circle, trace the bottom of the large cup. Then cut out both circles.

2. Fasten each paper circle on a piece of cloth with a straight pin. Cut around the edge of each paper circle to make two circles of cloth, one large and one small. Remove the pins and paper and put them aside.

3. Thread the needle and tie a knot at the end so that the thread won't pull out of the fabric. Make tiny stitches around the edge of the small piece of cloth. When you've stitched around the entire circle of fabric, carefully pull the thread tight. The fabric will gather up into a small bunch. Tie off the extra thread with the needle and cut off the remaining strand.

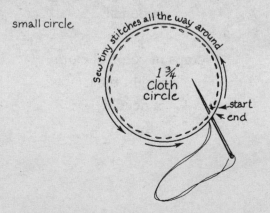

small circle

Sew tiny stitches all the way around

1 ¾"
Cloth
circle

start
end

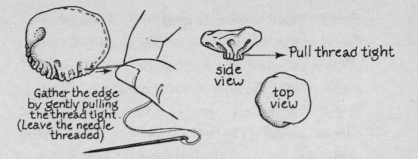

Gather the edge
by gently pulling
the thread tight.
(Leave the needle
threaded)

side
view

Pull thread tight

top
view

4. Turn under the edge of the large circle of cloth
and stitch all the way around. Pull the thread and
gather up the fabric as you did with the small circle. There will be a small hole left in the center.
Tie off the thread and cut it loose.

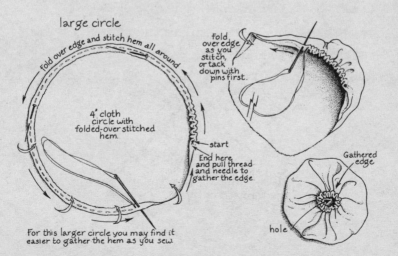

large circle

Fold over edge and stitch hem all around

Fold
over edge
as you
stitch,
or tack
down with
pins first.

4" cloth
circle with
folded-over stitched
hem.

start

End here
and pull thread
and needle to
gather the edge.

Gathered
edge

hole

For this larger circle you may find it
easier to gather the hem as you sew.

5. This is the most complicated step. If you need extra help, ask a grown-up. Take the small circle of cloth and push the end where the material is gathered into the hole in the large circle of cloth. Sew the two pieces together, so that the round part of the small circle is in the center of the large circle. Tie off the thread and cut it loose.

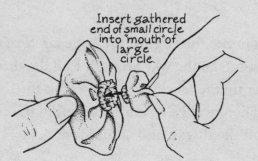

Insert gathered end of small circle into "mouth" of large circle.

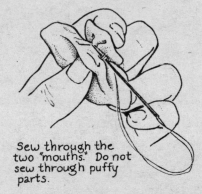

Sew through the two "mouths." Do not sew through puffy parts.

6. Fluff up the fabric and you will have a Doo-Lolly.

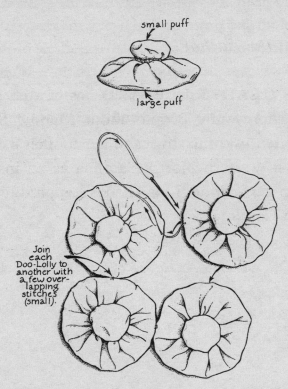

small puff

large puff

Join each Doo-Lolly to another with a few over-lapping stitches (small).

You can make long strips of Doo-Lollies by sewing the edges together. Use them for decoration by sewing them onto pillow tops, aprons, bedspreads, curtains, and clothes. You can make different sizes and colors for a rainbow effect!

About the Author

LOIS GLADYS LEPPARD has written many novels for young people about Mandie Shaw. She often uses the stories of her mother's childhood in western North Carolina as an inspiration in her writing. Lois Gladys Leppard lives in South Carolina.